DARK WATERS

Dark Waters
is published by Stone Arch Books,
a Capstone imprint
1710 Roe Crest Drive
North Mankato, Minnesota 56003
www.mycapstone.com

Cataloging-in-Publication Data is available on the Library of Congress website.

ISBN: 978-1-4965-4169-7 (library binding)
ISBN: 978-1-4965-4173-4 (paperback)
ISBN: 978-1-4965-4177-2 (eBook PDF)

Summary: India Finch is part-human and part-mermaid. In ocean water, special healing powers awaken in her, allowing her to help the merpeople. However, India longs for greater adventures than healing rashes, so when she hears rumors about Neptune's Trident, she decides to search for the powerful tool alongside her mermaid friends. The four friends soon find themselves facing off against dangerous and deadly mer who want Neptune's power for themselves.

Designer: Hilary Wacholz

Printed in the United States of America.
010019S17

DARK WATERS

NEPTUNE'S TRIDENT

A MERMAID'S JOURNEY

by JULIE GILBERT

illustrated by KIRBI FAGAN

STONE ARCH BOOKS
a capstone imprint

PREFACE

My name is India Finch. People say it's a funny name. India is a country, and a finch is a kind of bird. A country and a bird. It's an odd name for someone who is a mermaid. Well, part mermaid.

Confused? Me too. I didn't know I was part-mermaid until this summer. I'm spending the summer with my grandpa on the coast of Maine. It's beautiful here. Lots of pine trees and wild, rocky beaches. And the ocean is amazing. The sea stretches forever and ever. The waves crash against the rocks.

The ocean makes me feel huge and small at the same time. It feels like home.

I was shocked when Grandpa told me he was part-mer. I thought he was joking. Turns out he wasn't. Grandpa's mother was a mermaid. He's part-mer, and so am I.

On the outside, I look like an ordinary girl. I have medium brown skin, dark brown eyes, and crinkly dark hair. I get my stubborn chin from my mom and my crooked ears from my dad. I'm tall for my age, and my arms and legs are strong.

I look like an ordinary girl in the water too. When I'm in the ocean, I don't grow a tail or gills. But salt water makes my mer abilities wake up. I can breathe water instead of air. I can also swim for miles and miles without getting tired. And I can use my hands to heal injuries and illnesses. I have extra powers because I'm female. All mermaids have powers, but none of the mermen do.

My mermaid friends have amazing powers too.

Nari can talk to sea creatures using her mind. She can communicate with fish and lobsters and seals.

She says the sea creatures make better friends than most of the mer.

Dana can make water thick. When she does, I feel like I'm swimming in clear jelly. She likes to tease us sometimes. We'll be swimming along, and suddenly the water is too thick to move.

Lulu can move currents and make waves. She's really strong, just like her personality. I shouldn't have favorites, but I like Lulu the best. She's a fighter, like me. Or at least how I want to be.

The mer used to live all over the oceans. That's why so many cultures have stories about mermaids, even though people don't believe in mermaids. It's funny that humans don't know the mer are real. Humans are to blame for so many mer problems, after all.

Mer homes have always been protected by domes. The domes are like giant snow globes that make whatever is inside them invisible. The dome forms naturally when the mer live in harmony with their surroundings. Once people started drilling for oil, laying cables, and polluting oceans, mer homes were destroyed. The domes protecting the mer collapsed.

The mer started to die out. The remaining mer banded together and formed two tribes. Even though the tribes don't always get along, the mer are safer together than apart.

Almost three hundred mer live in these two tribes in the canyons off the coast of Maine. My mermaid friends are part of the Ice Canyon tribe. The other tribe is the Fire Canyon tribe. Neither tribe likes humans.

The Ice Canyon tribe wants to leave the humans alone. Live and let live, they say. The Fire Canyon mer are different. They want to attack humans and punish them.

Members from the different tribes aren't supposed to hang out with each other. This means I can't spend as much time with Evan as I'd like to. He's one of the Fire Canyon mer. He's also really smart — and cute. He seems to like me too.

I don't know how long I'll be able to hang out with Evan or any of my friends. Grandpa told me that when he was a young man, he had to choose between living on land or in the sea.

He had fallen in love with my grandmother. She was human. Because of her, Grandpa chose land. But he promised that his children and grandchildren would always help the mer.

Unfortunately my dad wanted nothing to do with the mer. He used to swim with them when he was my age, but then something happened. Dad made a bad decision, and a mermaid died. I don't know the whole story and neither does Grandpa.

When he was old enough, Dad moved to the middle of the country. Grandpa said Dad wanted to keep me away from the ocean while I was growing up. As a kid, I never knew I was part-mer. But I think Dad wanted me to know. Right before I got on the plane, Dad took me by the shoulders.

"Trust Grandpa," he said. "Whatever he says. No matter how crazy it sounds."

Then he hugged me tight and walked away.

I didn't know what Dad meant until I came to Maine and discovered my mer abilities. I still don't know if my mom knows. Even if Dad told her, I'm not sure she'd believe him.

The first time I talked with Dad on the phone, I asked him about the mer. I told him how shocked I was to learn the news. And that I wanted to know everything.

"We'll talk about it when you get home," was all he said.

I like being with the mer. They call me when they need my help by sending a seaweed wreath. Then I jump into the ocean to be with my friends.

Because I'm half-human, the dome makes it impossible for me to find the canyons on my own. The canyons are invisible to me until I'm inside the dome.

My human eyes can't see the dome, either, although it's supposed to be beautiful. My friends have to take me to and from the canyons where the mer live.

We have lots of wild adventures. Sometimes, though, I wonder if the mer only like me because of my powers. After all, I'm the only one who has healing powers. Would they even want me around if I couldn't help them?

I also wonder what my future holds. Will I have to make the same choice Grandpa did? Will I have to choose between my human side and my mermaid side? I'm not sure. I don't know which side I'd pick.

Maybe one day I'll know for sure.

CHAPTER 1

The letters sit on the blanket next to me. I glance at them every so often. Then I look out to sea. The sun is out for the first time in days. The light shimmers on the rolling waves, and the sand is warm between my toes. The scent of salt water drifts through the air.

I stretch out on the blanket. An old beach umbrella flutters over my head. I look at the letters again. They don't belong to me. I shouldn't have read someone else's mail. Even if this mail has been hiding beneath a floorboard in my room for years.

I found the letters two days ago in the middle of the night. I had to pee, so I went to the bathroom. On the way my foot caught on a nail. I was fumbling for a Band-Aid when I noticed the floorboard was loose.

No wonder it squeaked so much. I had avoided stepping on it for weeks. The squeak was so loud that you could hear it through the entire cabin. But I guess that's not saying much. Grandpa's cabin is tiny. I'm just happy I have my own room.

The next morning, I borrowed a hammer from Grandpa's toolshed. He was already gone to the marine sanctuary where he volunteers. I lifted the floorboard to shift it back in place. Then I saw the stack of grimy letters.

There were about a dozen of them, written by my dad to Grandpa. The first few were written before I was born. In them, Dad tells Grandpa about life in Ohio.

He describes his job at the college. He talks about Mom and her paintings. I skim over these. The one I read again and again is the last one.

Dear Dad,

You'll be happy to know your granddaughter was born last night. Mother and child are doing fine. We named the baby India.

She is beautiful. She has clouds of dark hair and is the color of caramel. Elise and I already love her more than anything.

I'm sure you understand why we won't come to Maine. I never wanted to be part-mer. And I never want to return to the ocean. But I can't make that choice for India. When she's eighteen, I'll send her to you. Then you can teach her. Until then, it's best if we don't visit. You are always welcome to visit us in Ohio.

I hope you understand.

Your son, Jamal

I'm so confused. Why did my parents send me to Maine this summer? I'm still fourteen, not eighteen. I mean, I know why they sent me away. They're fighting all the time. But why Maine? I could have gone to visit Mom's family in Colorado. And why now?

It turns out Grandpa doesn't like to fly, and he doesn't own a car. That's why he never came to visit us, either. When I got here at the beginning of June, Grandpa was as much a stranger to me as I was to him. But we've managed. I've learned so much this summer already. A lot of it is because of Grandpa.

"What have you got there?" Grandpa's gravelly voice breaks into my thoughts.

I jump and drop the letter.

"Holy cow, Grandpa, you scared me," I say. I scurry to pick up the letters and slip them under the beach towel.

"What are you doing out here?" Grandpa asks.

"Getting some sun," I say. "How did you know I was here?"

Grandpa points at the umbrella. "What else are you doing here?" he asks.

"Um . . . swimming?" I say.

"India," he says.

"Fine, I'm waiting for my friends. They haven't sent me a wreath in days," I explain.

Grandpa hunches down on the beach towel.

"I told you they might not call you again," he says. "The Finches help the mermaids when they are in trouble. But they might not need your help the rest of the summer."

I feel deflated, like a balloon that popped. "Maybe they'll just want to hang out."

"We don't hang out with the mermaids," Grandpa says. He says "hang out" like he's never said the words before. He probably hasn't. Grandpa is very formal for someone who lives alone in a tiny cabin on the beach.

"But why not?" I ask, not for the first time.

"It has never been the way things work," he says. He's never offered another explanation.

"I don't belong with them," I say. "Not really." The words slip from my mouth. It's the first time I've said it out loud.

Grandpa grunts, which means he's heard me.

We sit in silence for a long time. The waves rush against the sand. Then they are sucked back into the ocean.

"I don't belong in Ohio," I continue. My hands flop in my lap. "I don't belong here. And I don't belong with the mermaids. Most of them hate it when I show up."

Maybe they don't hate me, though, I reflect. I have helped them in the past. And I'll keep helping them, if they want. But for some of the mer, I look too human for them ever to *like* me.

"It is too dangerous to go by yourself," Grandpa repeats. "You can't find the canyons on your own. You must only go to the mermaids when there is trouble. They'll learn that you are there to help."

"And that I'll leave once I solve their problems," I grumble.

"Yes," Grandpa says.

We go back to watching the waves for a while. A few empty soda bottles bob in the water. I'll grab them later. It makes me angry to see garbage on the beach. *This is why the mermaids hate humans,* I think.

Eventually I ask, "Grandpa, why did Mom and Dad send me here?" I've been wanting to ask him ever since I read Dad's letter.

"Ah, so, you've been reading your father's letters," Grandpa says.

"I . . . what? No. What letters?" I say, scrambling to cover my tracks.

"The ones you were reading when I arrived. The ones that are hidden under the towel." Grandpa does not sound angry, only tired.

"Oh. Those letters," I say, pulling them out from beneath me. "I found them a few nights ago."

"I'd forgotten I'd put them in your room," Grandpa says. "I put them there years ago."

"I'm sorry I read them," I say.

"Are you?" he asks.

"Dad said he didn't want me to know about being a mermaid until I was eighteen," I say.

"Yes," Grandpa says.

I wait a full minute. "And?" I finally say. "I'm fourteen."

Grandpa shrugs, his narrow shoulders moving beneath his thin shirt. "Things change, India."

"Did Dad know you were going to tell me? About being part-mer?" I ask.

"What do you think?" Grandpa asks.

I hate when adults say that.

"When I got on the plane, he told me to trust you," I say. "No matter what you said. So he must have known I'd go into the ocean. And that you'd tell me about being a mermaid."

"He knew," Grandpa says. "When he called to tell me you were coming, I told him I would tell you."

"What did he say?" I ask.

"He said he wouldn't object," Grandpa says.

"Does Mom know about the mermaids?" I ask.

"Your mom wouldn't understand," he says.

I don't like how Grandpa dismisses Mom. "What do you mean?" I demand. "Mom's pretty cool." *Ugh, I can't believe I said that out loud,* I think.

"Your mom is not the kind of person who would understand," Grandpa says.

"That's not fair," I say.

"She lacks magic in her soul," Grandpa says.

I open my mouth to argue, but I know deep down Grandpa is right. My mom is great, but she would never understand mermaids. Maybe that's one of the reasons Mom and Dad are fighting.

"So why did they send me here? Especially if Dad didn't want me to know until I was eighteen?" I ask. My question is still unanswered.

Grandpa traces his finger through the sand. "Honestly, India? I don't know."

"You don't?" I ask.

"All I know is that your Dad called me up at the marine sanctuary one day," Grandpa shares. "He asked if you could live with me for the summer. I said yes."

"But you didn't ask why?" I ask.

Grandpa's smile is crooked and sad.

"I had never met my granddaughter," he says. "I wasn't going to ask questions. I didn't want your dad to change his mind."

"Oh," I say. Grandpa never hugs me. Sometimes I'm not sure if he even likes having me around. Maybe I was wrong.

"Your dad is getting older," Grandpa says. "And I know he and your mom have been struggling. Maybe he wanted you to know your past. To know me and the mermaids."

"Even if it is dangerous," I say.

Grandpa nods. "Even if it is dangerous," he repeats. "It's part of growing up."

"Okay," I say. I'm not sure what else to say. I've never thought about it like that. I suppose growing up means taking risks. I've taken plenty this summer already, so maybe I am growing up.

Grandpa is about to say more when I see something in the tide.

"Look!" I say. I'm already on my feet. The letters fall to the towel. I run down the shore to where a seaweed wreath floats in the water. It's what I've been waiting for.

I look for a pink tail fin. Dana is usually the one who comes. I don't see her, but I know I will see her soon. I walk back to Grandpa, the wreath in my hands.

"They sent the wreath." I grin. "My friends need my help. They need me."

As we walk back to the cabin, I pretend not to notice Grandpa's frown.

CHAPTER 2

I'm ready to go in no time. I don't need to pack a suitcase or bring a lunch. I bring nothing except for the clothes I'm wearing. The mer will take care of everything else.

Soon I'm standing on the rocky point that juts into the ocean. Black, spiky rocks tower over the water. Waves crash roughly against them. The tides are tricky here. I have to jump clear of the rocks when I meet my friends. I also have to make sure no one sees me. If anyone saw me jump, they would call the police.

Grandpa came with me today, which is unusual. He doesn't usually see me off. "Be careful, India," he says.

I turn to look at him. For a second, he looks exactly like Dad. They have the same chocolate skin and close-cropped hair. Grandpa's face is older, of course. And his hair is white.

"I'll be fine, Grandpa," I say.

Grandpa clears his throat and takes a step toward me. "The business with your dad . . . ," he says. Then his voice trails off.

"What about it?" I ask.

"He's never accepted his mer past," Grandpa says. "He's been running from it for years. He's still running from it."

"I know," I say, although I'm not sure I really understand.

"But he sent you to me," Grandpa says. "Even though he knew I would tell you about the mermaids. I believe that deep down he wants you to understand your history."

"Even though he can't deal with it himself?" I ask.

"Maybe he will understand some day," Grandpa says. "Maybe you'll help him."

"Maybe," I say.

The breeze picks up. The sun is out but the wind is cool. I shiver.

"I should get going," I say.

"Yes, of course," Grandpa says. He puts a hand on my shoulder. It's as close as he usually gets to hugs. "Be safe, India."

"See you soon, Grandpa," I say. I pat his hand. Then I move to the edge of the rock. I swing my arms, just like I do before a swim race. Then I jump into the water.

I hate this part. My lungs struggle to breathe water instead of air. Salt stings my eyes. I always have a moment when I think it won't work, and I'll drown here.

Just like usual, however, I've adjusted within a matter of minutes.

The ocean is bright and warm today. My arms and legs feel strong, and soon I'm swimming in the direction of Ice Canyon. I've been there enough times that I know to swim east.

Usually I start swimming toward Ice Canyon, and my friends come to meet me. Even if I could find my way there alone, I can't cross into the canyon on my own because of the guards. Some of them like me enough to let me in. But others would block my way.

Grandpa's face flashes through my mind as I swim. It reminds me of when he first told me I was a mermaid. It was right after I arrived. I will never forget it.

I never thought mermaids were real. Not once. Not even when I got to Maine and saw the ocean. On my first day, Grandpa marched me to the edge of the beach. He shoved a wreath of wildflowers into my hands.

"It's for them," he said.

"For who, Grandpa?" I asked.

"For the mermaids," Grandpa said.

I stared at him. Was Grandpa crazy? Did I need to call 911?

"Every summer I give the mermaids a gift. A reminder of my promise," he said, gazing out to sea.

"Um, okay, Grandpa," I said. I decided to play along. Isn't that what people do in movies? When they think the other person is nuts? "What promise?"

"I worry you're too young to understand," he said after a long pause.

"I'm not," I protested. "I'm fourteen. You can tell me, Grandpa."

Grandpa looked at me as if he were seeing me for the first time. "Maybe you are ready."

"Then tell me," I demanded.

"No more questions for now," he said. "Tomorrow I will explain everything. Throw the wreath, India." He nudged my shoulder. His hand was dark brown against my purple shirt. My skin was only a few shades lighter than his.

"Throw it," he repeated. I tossed the wreath into the ocean. What else was I supposed to do?

I watched the wreath bob and float on the waves. Then I followed Grandpa back to his cabin. He did not answer any of my questions. After a while I stopped asking. That night, my hands smelled like lily of the valley.

I went back the next day to see if the flowers had washed up on the rocks. The tide should have brought them back. I walked up and down the shore for hours, but I never found the wreath.

When I was leaving, though, I saw something in the waves. It was a flash of silver. It looked like a large tail fin.

Probably a shark, I thought. At least that's what I told myself. I pretended I hadn't seen a burst of red hair.

That night Grandpa told me the whole story. That's when everything changed.

Grandpa didn't like using electricity, so the cabin glowed with candles. I was using a flashlight to read my book. Normally I would be online, but my phone didn't work at the cabin.

"It's time," Grandpa said.

I snapped my book shut. "Time for what?" I asked.

"Time for you to know about the promise I mentioned the other day. And your history," he said, sitting at the table.

"Oh, that," I said.

"Yes, that," Grandpa said, clearing his throat. "I don't know how to say this. I guess I will just say it." He adjusted his glasses, peering at me over the rims. "My mother was a mermaid."

"Um, what?" I asked, figuring I hadn't heard him right.

"My mother was a mermaid," Grandpa repeated slowly.

"Grandpa, did you have a beer with dinner?" I joked. Maybe he was crazy.

Grandpa sighed. "I am not drunk, India. I am telling you about your family. My mother was a mermaid. She loved my dad. He was human. I'm part-mer."

"What?" I repeated. This whole thing was so weird.

"Your great-grandmother was a mermaid. Your dad and I are both part-mer." Grandpa cleared his throat again. "And you're part-mer too."

I put my book down, shaking my head. My curls danced through the air.

"No, that can't be right. I'd have a tail, for one," I said, reaching for whatever logic I could find.

"Your human traits are stronger than your mer traits," Grandpa said. "We look human both on land and in the sea. But if we dive deep into the ocean, we can breathe and see everything clearly underwater."

I didn't believe him.

"How come I've never noticed this before?" I asked. "I swim all the time. I'm on the swim team at school. I was even supposed to go to swim camp this year."

"You've never swum in the ocean before," Grandpa said. "Only salt water turns you into a mermaid."

"Do I grow a tail too?" I was joking at this point.

Grandpa wasn't. "No. Only full mermaids have tails. But you can swim very fast in salt water. Faster than humans."

I shook my head. "This doesn't make sense, Grandpa. If I was a mermaid —"

"Part mer," Grandpa interrupted.

"Fine. If I was part-mer, I would have noticed," I insisted.

"Here," Grandpa said. He pulled a photograph from beneath the table. The edges were curled, and the image was in black and white.

My eyes immediately found the woman at the center of the picture. She lay on a beach, her head propped in her hands. She smiled at the camera. She had dark skin and looked just like Grandpa and Dad.

Below her waist, she didn't have legs. Instead, she had a fish tail.

"This can't be real," I said.

"It is real," Grandpa said. "That's my mother."

"No," I was starting to believe him, and it scared me. "How is that even possible?"

Grandpa cleared his throat. "They weren't married, of course. They couldn't even live together. But my dad spent every day at the shore with my mom."

"But . . . but she's a . . . she's a . . ." I couldn't even say the word mermaid. But I couldn't ignore her tail in the photo.

"Yes, she was a mermaid," Grandpa said. "And she loved my dad and me."

"What happened?" I asked.

"She died," Grandpa said. "When I was a boy."

"How did she die?" I asked.

"She got sick. Then she died," he said gruffly.

"If you're part-mer, why don't you live in the ocean?" I asked. I crossed my arms over my chest and slouched in my chair.

"I had to choose," Grandpa said. "I met your grandma, and I fell in love. I chose her."

"So you never go back to visit the mermaids?" I asked.

"It was too hard as I got older," Grandpa explained. "I couldn't be a part of the mer tribes and be here with my human family at the same time. So I chose the land."

I had a headache. I didn't really believe Grandpa's story. Or at least I didn't want to believe him.

I dropped the picture on the table. "I've heard enough," I said. "I'm going to bed, Grandpa."

Grandpa gripped the edge of the table, but his voice remained calm. "Good night, India. Tomorrow we will go to the ocean again. I will prove that I'm not lying," he said.

I went to my small bedroom and laid down without even brushing my teeth. Grandpa's words rang in my head, even though I tried to block them. When I slept, I dreamed of mermaids.

The next morning, we went to the rocks. Grandpa pushed me into the water. Only then did I discover that what he said was true. I was part-mer.

CHAPTER 3

"India!"

The water churns as my friends all reach me at once. We are laughing and hugging, talking over each other in our excitement.

"Okay, enough," Lulu says, taking charge like she always does. Her voice cuts through the noise. "Let's give India some space."

"So how are you?" Dana asks. Her red hair fans around her rosy cheeks. She nudges me playfully on the arm. "You got my wreath?"

"I did," I say. "I was so happy to get it. I've missed all of you."

"We missed you too," Nari says. Her black hair is shiny and straight. She has a sapphire blue tail with sparkly diamond fins.

"They did, at least," Lulu says, teasing me.

"Same," I say with a grin. Lulu looks most like me. Her brown skin is a few shades darker than mine, and her hair is a thick, gorgeous mass of black curls. Her tail is green with yellow fins.

I kick my legs. "So where are we going?"

"To see my mom," Lulu says. She starts swimming in the direction of Ice Canyon, and we all follow.

Lulu's mom, Ani, is the leader of the Ice Canyon tribe of mermaids. All of my friends — with the exception of Evan — are members of the Ice Canyon tribe. I guess that sort of makes me a member too. Or at least it would if the other Ice Canyon members liked me.

"What's been happening in Ice Canyon?" I ask as we approach the huge cliffs that mark the canyon.

"Nothing too exciting," Lulu says. "Mom will tell you more."

"Okay," I say as we reach the edge of the canyon. We pass by the guards, who groan when they see me. These guards only let me pass because I'm with my friends.

Things aren't very different when we swim into the wide crevasses of the canyon. The mer live in caves all through the enormous cliffs. Several of them peek out at me but don't smile. One or two give a short wave. It seems a few mer remember the ways I've helped them in the past. I guess this is a start.

The canyons are beautiful and huge, larger than the Grand Canyon. I tried swimming straight to the top once, and it took me more than ten minutes. Coral covers the rocks in patches of blue and purple and red. When I'm here, I can't think of any place more beautiful.

"India!" Ani says as we reach her cave. She greets me with a hug.

"Hi, Ani," I say. It's strange to call a grown-up by her first name. The mer don't have last names, though.

"Come in, come in," Ani says. She leads us into her large cave. Several mer have been meeting with her. She dismisses them with a nod of her head. Soon my friends and I are alone with Ani.

"India, how has your summer been?" she asks.

"It's been fine," I say. "I've really liked the time I've spent here. I wish I could spend more —"

"We're glad you're back," Ani says, interrupting me. She always does that when I ask about visiting more. "We have a problem."

"What is it?" I ask, feeling a rush of excitement.

Ani leans forward and clasps her hands. "Have you ever heard of scallop scab?"

"Um, no . . . ," I say. As far as I know, scallop scab isn't a thing on land.

"It's a mild but annoying condition," Ani explains. "A series of raised red bumps form on the skin in the shape of a scallop. It is itchy and very catchy. A quarter of the tribe has it so far."

"Is it deadly?" I ask, waiting for the exciting part.

Ani looks confused. "No. As I said, it is a mild condition. Red, itchy bumps."

"So it's a skin rash," I say.

"Yes," Ani confirms.

"You brought me down here to heal a skin rash?" The words slip out before I can stop them.

Ani lifts her head and looks down her nose at me. I immediately feel ashamed.

"It's not the most exciting task," Ani says. "But you're the only one with healing abilities in the tribe right now. Not every task can be thrilling."

"I'm sorry," I say. "I can help."

"Good," Ani nods. She swims toward the door and dismisses us.

"Can India stay with us?" Lulu asks.

"Of course," Ani says.

I'm happy to hear this. Lulu, Dana, and Nari have their own cave. All the mer do from an early age. I love staying with them. It's like having an endless slumber party.

"Should I get started right away?" I ask.

"That would be best," Ani says. "The girls can set you up in an empty cave. I will have my aides start sending mer to you soon."

"Okay, thanks," I say.

Ani catches my hand. "I know it's not easy coming down here only to work," she says. She is close enough that my friends can't hear. "And I wish you could visit more often. It's just not always safe."

"I understand," I say.

And I do. I just wish it were different. I wish the mer could accept me for who I am — human *and* mer. And I wish I understood what it means for me to be both.

I push these thoughts away and follow my friends to an empty cave.

CHAPTER 4

Scallop scab is gross. The rash starts on the arms and then spreads across the back and onto the tail. The clusters of red bumps are thick and ooze pus. The itching is the worst thing about it, the mer say. Fortunately, scallop scab is easy to heal.

"Thanks," a mermaid says as she leaves the cave with a swish of purple tail. At least this one talked to me. Most of the mer give me a nod at most.

"Next!" I call.

"Are they always that rude?" Lulu asks, swimming into the room. "She was the last one, by the way."

"She was a nice one," I say.

"Not cool," Lulu says, frowning after the mermaid.

"We might as well face it. The Ice Canyon mer will never accept me as one of their own," I say.

Lulu tilts her head. "Do you want to be one of us?"

"Um, uh . . . yeah," I say.

"Why?" Lulu asks.

I try to read Lulu's face. *Is she making fun of me?* I wonder.

"Are you teasing me?" I ask.

"Of course not," Lulu says. "Why would you think I'm teasing you?"

"Being a mermaid would be awesome," I say. "Why wouldn't I want to be one of you?"

Lulu shrugs her shoulders. "You'd have to leave your old life behind."

"Why couldn't I do both? Live on land and also come to the sea sometimes?" This question has been bothering me for weeks. Grandpa chose to stay on land. But that was because he fell in love with my grandmother, who was fully human.

"Loyalty is very important to the mer," Lulu says. "We need to know that the mer come first. No matter what. That's why they haven't fully accepted you."

"They want me to choose," I say.

"Yeah," Lulu says.

I place a hand against the smooth wall of the cave and kick my legs now and again to stay in place. "Who says mer and humans have to be at odds?" I ask. "What if humans have the same goals at the mer?"

"Like what?" Lulu asks, giving me the side eye.

"A lot of humans want clean oceans too," I say.

"All of them?" Lulu asks.

"Well, no," I admit.

"Ice Canyon or Fire Canyon doesn't matter in this case," Lulu says. "The mer have one shared goal. We want our homes to be safe."

"Humans want that too," I say.

"The problem is," Lulu says, "most humans don't see the ocean as their home."

Her words sink in the water between us. I know she's right. And it makes me sad.

There's some motion behind us. Another mermaid has arrived with scallop scab.

"I should go," Lulu says. She gives me a quick hug. "We'll figure it out, India."

I hope she's right, I think as I wave the next mermaid into the cave.

A dozen other mer come to me that afternoon. I heal all of them. I hover my hands over the area with the scallop scab, close my eyes, and think of how water heals. I think about how water washes things clean. I channel those thoughts through my hands. I can't fully explain what happens next. Somehow my thoughts get turned into healing powers. Those powers clear up the scallop scab.

By the time the last mer leaves, I'm tired. I swim slowly toward my friends' cave, stopping when I hear voices coming from Ani's cave. I don't like to spy on people. I only stop because the voices sound like arguing. At least that's what I tell myself.

I creep near the edge of the cave and make sure no one inside can hear me. Then I hunch down to listen.

"Neptune's Trident? You can't be serious," Ani is saying.

"The reports are convincing," another voice growls. I know this voice. It belongs to Storm, the leader of the Fire Canyon tribe and Evan's dad.

"They are rumors, not reports," Ani says. "Neptune's Trident was only ever a legend."

"How can you be so sure?" Storm asks.

"Please. A magical spear that the god of the sea used to have?" Ani snorts. "A weapon that can stir up major storms? A weapon that can create tidal waves? That's silly."

"Most humans would say mermaids are nothing more than legend," Storm replies.

"You're not really sending mer to look for it, are you?" Ani asks.

"I have to," Storm says. "If Fire Canyon has control of the trident, it will help us."

There is a moment of silence.

"Help you how?" Ani finally asks.

"You know how," Storm grunts.

"You wouldn't use the trident against humans, would you?" Ani asks. "Or let me guess. Create tidal waves and storms to wash away the coast? Even you aren't that cruel, Storm."

"I have to do what is right for my tribe," Storm says. "They want the trident recovered, so we are going to look for it. If we find it, we will use it."

"You've told me you don't agree with your tribe. Remember? You said you have questions. And yet you'll still use the trident against humans?" Ani asks.

"I have to," Storm says. "My tribe will kick me out if I don't."

Ani grunts. "This is low, even for you," she says.

"The Fire Canyon tribe is loyal to me," Storm argues. "They are loyal to the idea of getting rid of humans. We need the trident to save the oceans."

"So why tell me?" Ani asks. "Why not find the trident on your own?"

"I . . . I wanted you to have a fair chance," Storm says.

"Why?" Ani asks.

I hear a rustling sound but no words.

"You don't want to use the trident to harm humans, do you?" Ani says eventually.

This time Storm groans. "It doesn't matter what I think. I am the leader of Fire Canyon, and I must do what my tribe wants me to do," he says.

"You are afraid of your tribe," Ani says.

"I am not afraid of them. But I must be loyal to them," Storm says. "They want to find the trident. So I will send mer to find it. They will bring it back to me. Then we will decide what to do."

"And you're telling me so I can send my own group," Ani says. "So the Ice Canyon mer can get the trident before your tribe. That way you don't have to make the choice yourself."

There is more silence.

"You are a coward," Ani says.

Storm ignores her words. "According to the last reports, the trident is underwater off the coast of Rose Island . . . in the Bahamas."

"I know where Rose Island is," Ani says. "I have a friend who lives nearby."

"And does this friend know about the trident?" Storm asks.

"I don't think so," Ani says. "I haven't talked to her in years, though. Maybe she knows something now."

"Will you send a group?" Storm asks.

Ani sighs. "I haven't decided yet. I need to think about it."

"Don't think too long," Storm says. "I'm sending a group to search for it. They leave the day after tomorrow."

"Very well," Ani says. "Good night."

I hide behind a rock as Storm sweeps past me. He doesn't see me. As I watch him leave, I think about how much he looks like his son, Evan.

My heart gives a flutter when I think about Evan. He's not my boyfriend. Or would it be merfriend? Anyway, we're not an item. But I like him. A lot. His dad doesn't like me, though. I'm too human.

I hear Ani swimming around her cave. She wouldn't like finding out I've been spying on her. I push thoughts of Evan out of my mind and quietly creep away.

As I swim to where my friends live, I can't wait to tell them about what I heard. They will love to know about the trident. And hopefully they'll think searching for it sounds much more exciting than healing a skin rash.

CHAPTER 5

I run into my friends on my way back to the cave. I don't get a chance to tell them about what I've heard.

"We were just coming to find you. We're heading to the *Clemmons,*" Nari says.

"You-know-who might be there," Lulu says.

I don't need to hear their laughter to know I'm blushing.

"Race you there!" Dana says. She sprints ahead, and the others race after her. I'll tell them about the trident later.

"Wait for me!" I call, swimming as fast as I can. I almost catch them before we reach the *Clemmons*.

The *Clemmons* is my favorite place in the Canyons. The wreck of the steamship lies on its side on the bottom of the ocean. A hundred years ago, it carried passengers across the ocean. Now it's a hangout for the younger mer of both tribes. The younger mer don't care as much about the tribe distinctions. Some of them even think there should only be one tribe. Most of them like me too.

I also love the *Clemmons* because it usually means I get to see Evan.

A big group lounges on the deck already. Some mer throw shells back and forth. They swim between a couple of large rocks as some kind of mer game. They tried to explain it to me once, but it's more complicated than it looks.

Evan is playing the shell game. He's laughing, and his dark hair floats in the water. I love that he's smiling. He's normally so serious. He has a hard time as Storm's son because Evan doesn't want to hurt humans.

Although it sounds like Storm doesn't either, I think, remembering the conversation I overheard at Ani's cave.

"And look who's here. Lucky us," Dana says, frowning.

A tiny mermaid with bright blond hair and a swishy ice blue tail swims up to Evan. She giggles and puts her hand on his shoulder. I cringe.

"Melody," I say.

"Yep," Lulu replies.

"Have they been hanging out a lot?" I ask, trying to sound like I don't care.

"Not a lot," Dana says. "Usually he ignores her."

"He's not ignoring her today," I say.

"Evan!" Lulu shouts. "Evan!" She waves until he looks over. "Look who's here!" She points at me.

I want to hide under a rock. Everything changes when Evan sees me, though. His smile gets even bigger. He drops the shell and swims over to us. Over his shoulder, I see Melody glaring at us.

"India, you're back," Evan says. I always forget how cute he is. He has light brown skin and a violet tail. His dark eyes make my knees weak.

"Yeah, I am," is all I say. I could kick myself. *Say something else,* I tell myself.

Dana beats me to it. "How's the game?"

"Fine. We're winning," Evan says.

"Don't let us keep you," I say without thinking.

Why did I say that? I wonder. I don't want him to go back to the game and to Melody.

"We're almost done," Evan replies. "Let me finish, and then I'll find you."

"Okay," I say. We swim over to the bottom of the ship. Several mer wave to me or say hi.

"That was —" Lulu starts to say. I know she is going to comment on what I said to Evan.

"Don't say it," I say. I change the subject. "Have any of you ever heard of Neptune's Trident?"

"The trident? Sure," Dana says.

"You have?" I am surprised. Storm made it sound like it was a secret.

"My parents told me all kinds of trident stories when I was a kid," Nari says.

"What do you know about it?" I ask.

"Well, it has all kinds of magical properties," Nari says. "It can create lightning underwater."

"It's supposed to be able to create huge storms," Dana adds.

"Ani used to tell me that the trident could rip through water. If you threw it, it would go for miles before stopping," Lulu says. "Why are you asking?"

"Well, I kind of did something I wasn't supposed to," I say. I twist a strand of hair around my finger — a nervous habit.

"What did you do?" Dana asks.

"I eavesdropped on your mom," I say to Lulu.

"Who was she talking to?" Lulu asks. She doesn't seem bothered that I was spying.

"She was talking to Storm about the trident," I announce. My words do not have the impact I hope. My friends look confused, not excited.

"So?" Lulu asks.

"Storm heard rumors that the trident is real," I explain. "He said it's near Rose Island in the Bahamas."

"The Bahamas are thousands of miles from here," Dana points out.

"Storm thinks the trident is real and that if he has it, he can create storms. He wants to wipe out the coastal cities," I say.

My friends stare at me.

"Well, to be honest, Storm wasn't sure if he would use it," I admit. "But his tribe wants him to get it so he's sending a group to Rose Island. He said he would decide once he had the trident. But he thinks it's real."

"Why was he telling my mom?" Lulu asks.

"She asked him that too," I say. "I think he's hoping Ani will send mer to find it. If someone else finds it first, Storm won't have to make a decision."

"Is my mom sending a group?" Lulu asks.

"She said she had to think about it," I say.

"That means no," Lulu says. She pushes away from the side of the ship and swims back and forth. If she had legs, she'd be pacing.

"How do you know?" I ask.

"Mom always says she has to think about it when she means no," Lulu says.

"That's funny," I say. "My mom does the exact same thing."

"So she's not sending anyone to find the trident. But Storm is. If Storm's mer find the trident, they will use it against humans." Lulu keeps swimming in front of us.

"Lulu," Dana says. Her voice has a warning tone.

"What?" I ask.

"I know what she's thinking," Dana says. "And it's a terrible idea."

"How is it a terrible idea?" Lulu asks.

"How is it not?" Dana responds. She doesn't sound mad, just worried.

"It's thousands of miles," Nari says.

"Thousands of miles of adventure," I say. "We'd have so much fun."

"It would be fun," Dana admits.

"We can't," Nari says.

"Can't do what?" Evan asks, surprising us as he swims up to our group.

"We can't swim past the Breakers," Lulu says. She points past the *Clemmons* toward a spot in the ocean where the tides get rough. Because of the dangerous currents, the Breakers are off-limits to the mer.

"Why would you want to swim past the Breakers?" Evan asks. Then something clicks in his eyes. "Wait, are you searching for the —" His voice breaks off.

A shimmer of worry slides through my stomach. "Searching for what?" I ask.

"Nothing," Evan says. He looks uncomfortable. "I'm not supposed to talk about it."

"Is it the trident?" I ask.

Evan stares at me. "How did you know about the trident?"

I shrug. "We're not supposed to talk about it, either."

"You're not going after it too, are you?" Evan asks.

"We haven't decided yet," Lulu says.

"Is Melody going with you?" I ask. The question slips from my mouth.

Evan looks confused. "What does Melody have to do with this?"

"Nothing," I say, blushing.

"We don't think the trident is real," Nari says. She folds her arms across her chest. She looks both brave and scared at the same time.

"To tell you the truth, I'm not sure it is real," Evan says.

"Why go after it, then?" I ask.

"My dad," Evan says. His voice trails off. "He wants it."

"The trident is supposed to have terrible powers," I say. "It's supposed to cause storms and tidal waves."

"I've heard that too," Evan says. He doesn't meet my eyes.

"If the Fire Canyon tribe gets the trident, they will use it to hurt humans," I continue.

Evan gives his head a shake. "They won't."

"You don't know that," Nari says. "They might use the trident to hurt India's grandfather."

Evan gives me a fierce look. "I won't let that happen."

I swim toward him then. We are floating so close our noses almost touch. I could kiss him if I wanted to. I meet his eyes instead.

"Don't make promises you can't keep," I say. Then I swim away.

By the time Nari, Dana, and Lulu catch up with me, I've wiped the tears from my face.

My friends don't say anything until we reach their cave.

Nari breaks the silence. She starts swimming around the cave, pulling out packs of seaweed.

"Nari, what are you doing?" I ask.

She gives me a quick smile, even though her eyes are serious. "What does it look like I'm doing? I'm gathering supplies," she says.

"You want to go?" I ask, feeling suddenly excited.

Nari gives me another smile. "When do we leave?"

CHAPTER 6

We leave at dawn the next morning. We don't have much to carry. My friends hand me a backpack woven from seaweed. Inside are packets of seaweed to eat. The Ice Canyon mer are picky eaters and only like the seaweed from this canyon. I never bring anything from home when I visit. So I guess I'll be wearing these clothes for a while.

As we sneak away from Ice Canyon, I think about Grandpa. I doubt he would approve of me swimming fifteen hundred miles to the Bahamas. The distance is roughly the same as walking from Maine to Iowa. But technically Grandpa didn't say I *couldn't* swim to the Bahamas, so I guess I'm okay.

As we swim past the canyons, I find myself looking for Evan. A part of me can't help thinking it would be really cool to be on this trip with him. But then I remember that his tribe wants the trident so they can hurt humans.

Can I like someone who wants to hurt people? How much does Evan agree with the Fire Canyon mer? Maybe he's like Storm. Maybe he wants the trident so he can keep it out of the hands of the mer who want to use it? The questions keep coming, and I'm lost in my thoughts for a while.

I hear Lulu say, "We need to get past the guards." I look up. We are almost at the edge of Ice Canyon.

"Tell them we're going on a picnic," I say.

"A what?" Lulu asks.

"A picnic," I explain. "Where you eat your food outside? Humans do it all the time when the weather is nice."

Lulu gives me a weird look. "India, we're always outside."

"What's your bright idea, then?" I grumble.

"Hush," Lulu says. "He'll hear you." The guard is swimming toward us.

"Going somewhere, ladies?" the merman asks in a gruff voice. He sounds mean, but he's not. I healed his scallop scab a few days ago. He sang me a few rusty bars of a song to thank me.

"We're just going for a picnic, Bruce," Lulu says.

"A picnic?" Bruce asks.

"You know, where we take our food and eat outside," Dana jumps in.

Bruce looks confused. "Isn't that what the mer always do?" he asks.

"Yeah, but we wanted to go further than Ice Canyon," Nari says. "It was India's idea."

I give a weak smile and wave.

"She's missing home," Lulu adds. "Humans often have picnics. We thought this might cheer her up."

I do my best to look homesick.

"Okay, then," Bruce says. "I'm not going to stop you. You should be fine. We haven't seen any sharks or squid in a few days. Be careful, though."

"Thank you!" we call as we swim past the southern border of Ice Canyon.

"That was easier than I thought," Lulu says once we are out of sight.

"Only after I gave you the picnic idea," I say.

"Thanks for that." She grins.

"It's nice to know there haven't been any sharks or squid," Nari says. She sounds a little worried, despite her bright tone. She should be. Sharks and squid are the two creatures that prey on mermaids.

"Look at how cool everything is!" Dana exclaims. "The water is so bright!" She grabs my arm. "And look at those green fish!"

"We've barely left Ice Canyon," I say. "You see fish like that all the time."

"I know, but doesn't everything look new? Isn't it exciting? Look at that rock over there." Dana points at a plain-looking rock.

"Looks like every other rock," I say.

"I know, but we've never see that rock before!" Dana says. "And look at that school of tuna."

She points to a cloud of silver fish ahead of us. We weave a path around them.

"No matter what happens on this trip, Dana's going to make it fun," Lulu says.

"You're welcome," Dana says with a laugh.

The sun is shining, and the waters are warm and bright. I'm with my friends, and we are having an adventure. I'm still hoping to see Evan on the trip. But even if I don't, that's okay. I stop thinking about him and have fun with my friends instead.

"Come on, India!" Dana calls. "Let's go and have some fun."

Over the first few days, we have a great time. The weather holds, and our trip is all sunshine and calm waters. We spend our days talking and swimming. At night we find safe places to rest. We don't see any sharks or squid.

On day three, I start to realize how far we are from home. We've swam for miles and miles, but we're still really far from where we're going.

We're just out here in the ocean, alone. I start to feel a little anxious. If anything happened to us, what would we do? Who would help us? I find myself glancing over my shoulder, looking for sharks. Nothing's ever there, but I can't help feeling like something's watching us. I don't want to ruin the trip, so I keep my worries to myself.

But eventually, they bubble over.

"Anyone know if there are sharks or squid in the Bahamas?" I ask one afternoon. We have paused near the top of a huge sea volcano. The base sinks down thousands of feet below us.

"Of course there are sharks and squid in the Bahamas," Lulu says. "There are sharks and squidseverywhere in the ocean."

"I was wondering if anyone knew about particular kinds," I clarify. "Is there anything in the Bahamas that's more dangerous than what we see in Maine?"

"I don't know," Lulu says.

"You don't know?" My eyebrows raise almost to my forehead. "Why don't you know?"

"Why *would* we know?" Lulu replies. "We swim, and we see what happens. That is the mer way."

"Didn't anyone check?" I ask. We're in the middle of nowhere. Rock cliffs surround us. I can't help but wonder what's lurking in those caves.

"How would we have checked?" Dana asks.

I don't have an answer. Sometimes I forget the mer don't have the Internet.

"Maybe you could have asked someone," I say.

"How would that have worked?" Dana asks. She pretends to hold a conversation with one of the mer: "'Hey, tell us about dangerous creatures in the Bahamas! Why are we asking? Oh, no reason."

"Don't you have legends and stuff?" I ask. "Stories about the Bahamas?"

"Sure we do," Nari says. "But I don't think any of them talk specifically about sharks or squid."

"Why are you so worried?" Dana asks.

"I'm not," I say. "But that guard, Bruce, told us to be careful, so I started wondering what might be out here."

We look around. Suddenly the sea seems creepy. A few days ago, I would have been wondering what excitement lay on the other side of the mountain. Now I'm afraid of what we might find.

"We *are* a long way from home," Nari says. Her voice wobbles a tiny bit.

"Everyone is probably missing us," Dana replies.

"Everyone is probably really angry at us," Nari corrects her.

My stomach sinks at her words. By now, Ani and everyone else at Ice Canyon knows we're gone. Bruce would have told them we were heading south. He thought it was for a picnic. But Ani will probably guess right away that we left in search of the trident. I hope she's not worried.

I hope Grandpa isn't worried, either. Especially if the trip takes longer than we thought. He doesn't mind when I have longer trips to the mer, but this will be the longest absence from home by far.

"We have to face it. We don't know what lies ahead," Dana says.

"Stop it, all of you," Lulu says. She swims in front of us. "India, this was your idea. We all wanted to go, but don't forget that this was your plan. We're not going back now. And don't worry about sharks or squid or anything. We have each other. We stick together, and we'll be fine."

Lulu glances overhead. The water glows the way it does at sunset.

"We can go a few more miles before we find a place to rest," she adds. "Tonight I'll check the stars again. We're on course to reach the Bahamas in about a week."

The mer might not know much about sea monsters in the Bahamas, but they do know how to read the stars. Lulu sticks her head above the surface every night. She knows which stars will lead us to Rose Island. We're going slightly west before we head south. If Ani does send anyone after us, they won't find us right away.

We follow Lulu deeper into the sea. I'm still a little afraid. I notice that Nari and Dana are holding hands. Suddenly I feel bad for making them scared.

"Lulu's right," I say. "I just got a little nervous. I haven't been this far from home before. But everything is fine. We have each other."

Even as I say it, though, I wonder if that will be enough.

CHAPTER 7

We're all in a better mood the next morning. The sun is shining again, and the waters are warm. I think we're near South Carolina. Or maybe it's still North Carolina. Either way, we are getting closer to Rose Island.

As we swim south, we are swimming against strong currents. To help us, Lulu creates pockets of smaller currents going the other way. These pockets help us swim against the stronger current. Lulu's pockets make the trip go faster.

"I love this," Dana says, floating by me. She's barely swimming.

"Watch this," Lulu says. She hands her pack of seaweed to Nari to hold and performs a fancy flip. She puts an extra burst onto the flip at the end, so she's sailing through the water.

"Cool!" Nari exclaims. She holds the packs close and does a somersault, ending with a pretty turn.

"That's nothing!" I say. I toss my pack at Nari. I fling my arms wide and do a cartwheel.

"Show off," Dana teases. "Just because you have legs."

I grin and shrug. Dana scrunches her face and motions me to get out of the way. I swim backward just in time.

Zoom!

Dana hurtles past me, spinning in a corkscrew.

"Sometimes tails are better," she says. Her cheeks are flushed, and her hair is tangled.

"You think that's something?" Lulu challenges. She shoots past us as well.

We spend the next half hour or so playing like this. We challenge each other to do bigger and bigger tricks. It's a fun way to pass the time. Until suddenly it isn't.

"Look at me," Nari says.

The rest of us have floated ahead, tired from our tricks. We're hungry, so maybe that's why we are ignoring Nari. "Let's get some rest at the next set of caves," Dana says.

"Sounds good," Lulu agrees.

"Hey, everyone, look at me!" Nari calls again.

This time she gets our attention. She is balancing on the tip of a dolphin's nose.

"No fair," we protest, laughing. None of us are able to include animals in our tricks.

"Watch," Nari says again. She nods to the dolphin, who tips its nose down. Then it snaps its head back, sending Nari spinning high in the water. Nari is doing all kinds of twists and turns in the water.

The trick should be simple. Nari should land near us, safe and sound. Instead, something else happens.

As we watch, Nari jumps. She does a flip, her arms outstretched. She's smiling. Her face is raised to the surface.

And then the current takes her.

In a flash, Nari is whipped away. The current tosses her back and forth. Her tail snaps, and her arms spin. Soon she's a blur racing past us.

"Nari!" Dana screams, clutching my hand.

Lulu is already moving, sending new currents to meet the strong one. But she's too late. Nari is already gone.

"No!" I'm shouting as the water carries Nari straight toward a rocky cliff. If she doesn't get out of the current, she will slam into it.

I hear someone scream. It takes me a moment to realize it was me.

Nari is screaming too. She puts out her hands to brace for impact. Dana's face is white. Lulu is shouting at the water, sending all kinds of currents toward Nari. I'm about to see my friend smash into a rock wall.

At the last moment, Lulu's currents catch Nari. They jerk her away from the wall just in time.

Dana's hand squeezes mine so hard that it hurts. Her eyes are squeezed shut.

"She's okay," I say. I put my arm around Dana. "Look, she's fine."

Dana opens her eyes and takes a shaky gulp of water. "She is?"

"Yes, look," I say. I point to Nari, who is making her way back to us. She looks like she is going to be sick.

Lulu reaches her first. She puts her arm around Nari. I'm surprised to see Nari brush Lulu away. Nari is always hugging us. She says something to Lulu. Lulu frowns. Then they make their way to us. Their faces are grim.

"What is it?" Dana asks. She reaches out to take Nari's hands.

"You . . . you all gave me your food packs when we were doing tricks," Nari says. She sounds like she's going to cry.

"So?" I say. I don't get what she's saying, but Dana understands.

"Oh, no," Dana says. We look at Nari's empty hands. She doesn't have any packs slung across her back, either.

"I'm sorry," Nari says. "The current hit me, and I got swept away. So did everything I was holding." She sniffles.

"So you're saying . . . ," I start. I need to hear it.

"I'm saying that we don't have any food," Nari says.

This is a big blow. Mermaids are picky eaters. They only eat a certain kind of seaweed that grows near Ice Canyon. When I'm in the ocean, I'm a picky eater too. I love all kinds of food on land, but in the ocean, I eat the same seaweed as the mer.

"What are we going to do?" Dana asks.

"We'll think of something," Lulu says. "We just have to keep going."

"We need food," Dana insists.

"I know that," Lulu says. Her voice is sharp.

"It's just that we're all going to be hungry soon," Dana adds.

I try to catch Dana's eyes to tell her to be quiet.

"We can't eat the seaweed that's out here," Dana continues. "I mean, we can try it, but it's disgusting. Do you want to go the rest of the way eating disgusting seaweed? Or no seaweed at all?"

"I will if it means you shut up!" Lulu snaps.

We stare at Lulu. Dana looks stunned. I know we are all tired and afraid after Nari's near accident. But Lulu's words are mean.

"That's not fair," Nari says. She takes Dana's hand.

"You want to talk about fair?" Lulu demands. "Fair is you not losing our food in the first place."

"You leave her out of this," Dana says. "She was only holding our food because you and India were showing off."

I wasn't angry before, but I am now. "I was showing off?" I say. "What about you and your tail spins? You were showing off just as much as me."

Lulu is shouting now too. "Don't forget that I'm the one who saved Nari in the first place! She's the one who tried a trick that was too much for her."

"It was too much for me?" Nari gasps. "I'm just as good a swimmer as you, and you know it, Lulu!"

"Then how come I had to save you?" Lulu snaps.

"That's totally not fair!" Dana protests. We are back to the beginning of our fight.

I have a moment where I almost stop the fight. I picture myself telling everyone to calm down. I lead us to shelter. Then I remind everyone that things will be better in the morning.

I've just opened my mouth when Lulu speaks again. "I didn't even want to come on this trip. The whole thing was India's idea. It's her fault."

Anger flares through me. "Are you kidding me?" I demand. "This is so not my fault. You all wanted to go on the trip too. It wasn't just me."

Lulu huffs and folds her arms across her chest. She looks so smug. Her expression makes me furious. I open my mouth and say the worst thing I could possibly say.

"You wanted to come more than I did. You want to bring the trident back to your mom. Maybe then she'd notice you for once," I spit.

Everyone gasps. Even I can't believe I said it. Lulu is touchy about her mom. She and Ani love each other, but Ani is usually so busy running Ice Canyon that she ignores Lulu. Honestly, I don't think it would make a difference if Ani weren't the leader. She would still be caught up in whatever she was doing.

Lulu's face looks gray. Her hands are trembling. I stare at her.

"Lulu, I'm so sorry, I shouldn't have said that. It was a terrible thing to say," I babble.

I wait for Lulu to say something. Anything. Finally she shakes her head. Her dark hair floats in the water.

"Let's keep going. There should be some caves up ahead," she says.

Dana and Nari nod.

"We need to keep our eyes open for seaweed too," Lulu says. Her voice is wooden. She swims away. I watch as Dana and Nari follow her.

I feel terrible. I'm the worst person in the world. For a second I think about turning back. Maybe it's best if I leave. I can't find Ice Canyon on my own, but maybe I could swim west toward the coast. I could call Grandpa to come get me.

An image of Grandpa's face floats through my mind. I can only imagine what he'd say when he learns I'm somewhere in the southern United States, having abandoned my friends.

I remember something Grandpa says often: "The mer are family. And family takes care of its own."

Mom and Dad are my family, even though they are fighting with each other. The mermaids are my family too. I'm the one who caused the fight. Or at least I'm the one who made it worse. I have to try to make it better, at least.

I turn south and follow my friends.

CHAPTER 8

Lulu doesn't make it easy for me to say I'm sorry.

By the time I catch up to the mermaids, they are huddled in a dark cave. Lulu stands guard at the entrance while Nari and Dana pick at a few strands of pale seaweed.

For a moment, I don't think Lulu is going to move.

"Can I come in?" I ask.

After a second, Lulu sniffs and inches to one side.

"Will you come in too? I want to talk to you," I say.

Dana and Nari watch us closely.

"I have to stand guard," Lulu says, not looking at me. "Anything you have to say, you can to say it here."

I take a deep breath. "Fine. I want to say I'm sorry. To all of you. But especially to you, Lulu. I didn't mean what I said about your mom. It's not true. I shouldn't have said it."

"Fine," Lulu says.

"Fine? What does that mean?" I ask.

Lulu finally looks at me. "I mean it's fine. You said what you wanted to say. Now get some rest."

"Okay," I say. I feel like I'm about three years old. I slide through the water to Nari and Dana, who give me grim looks.

"Here," Nari says. She pushes a few scraps of the pale seaweed into my hands. "It's all we could find."

"How does it taste?" I ask. I raise the seaweed to my nose. It stinks. I take a bite and gag. I manage to choke down a tiny mouthful.

"That's what we thought too," Dana says.

"I . . . um . . . I'm going to try to sleep," I say. I've had enough of the seaweed. I might as well go to bed. The day will be over sooner, at least.

"We are too," Dana says.

"Wake us for our shifts, Lulu," Nari says. "We are going to take turns guarding the cave," she tells me. "It was Lulu's idea."

"I'll take first shift," I say immediately. I have to do something to show I'm sorry.

"No worries. I've got it," Lulu says. She still doesn't look at me.

"No, really, I can do it," I say.

"India, no," Lulu says. "I'll take first watch. You sleep."

"But why?" I ask. I sound like I'm whining.

"Because I say so," Lulu says.

"Oh," I say. Lulu swims away to the entrance before I can say more.

It makes sense to take shifts. We're hundreds of miles from home. We have no idea what's out here. But I can't help thinking that taking shifts is also a way for Lulu to avoid talking to me.

I settle against a curve in the wall. Nighttime is when I miss being on land the most. I will never get used to floating in place to sleep. I miss my bed.

I miss my family and friends too, of course. I look around the cave. Dana and Nari are sleeping near each other. Lulu is outlined in the entrance to the cave. We are mad at each other, but these mermaids are my friends too. Even more than that, they are my family.

I sigh. Will I ever fit in as a mermaid? Do I want to live here all of the time?

Deep down I suspect the answer is no. I couldn't live here all of the time . . . not yet, at least. I want to finish high school and go to college and find a job that I love. Maybe after that, though. Maybe I will come back to live in the ocean when I'm old. I love the feel of the water on my skin, of knowing I can breathe it. I'm at home here.

Of course if I don't come back until I'm old, all of my mermaid friends will be old too. I will have missed their entire lives. I think of Evan. My heart stops. Maybe I can do both, live in the sea and on land.

Grandpa had to choose because of my grandma. It was too hard for him to live in both places. He had to pick. But what if I don't have to pick?

I hold this thought close as I drift into an uneasy sleep. The cave is cold. My stomach rumbles. I'm hungry, but there's nothing to eat.

I must fall asleep because suddenly Lulu is there, shaking me awake.

"You take the next watch. I'm tired," she says.

I follow her to the entrance of the cave. She starts to swim away, but I touch her wrist.

"Lulu, I'm so sorry," I say. "I know things aren't always good with your mom. I shouldn't have said it. And it's not true. Your mom notices you."

She pauses and turns back to me. "You know that's not really why I'm mad," she confesses.

"It isn't?" I ask.

"Not really. Sure, my mom gets caught up in her own stuff, and I have to work to get her attention." Lulu sighs and settles next to me against the wall. "Okay, so maybe I was a little mad about what you said." She laughs a little.

I grin in spite of myself. I'm happy that Lulu is talking to me.

"My mom wants me to take on more of her duties," Lulu says.

I don't understand for a moment. "Wait, like ruling-the-tribe kind of duties?"

Lulu nods. I watch her hair slide through the water. "She wants to train me to take over someday," she says. "When it's time."

"That's cool!" I say.

Lulu winces. I realize that was the wrong thing to say.

"Sorry," I say. "Do you not want to lead the tribe?"

Lulu gulps. When she speaks, the words come from deep down inside her. "No. I don't. At least I don't think so."

"What do you want to do?" I ask.

"That's the thing. I don't know," Lulu says. She wipes at her eyes. "My mom keeps saying that if I don't know, it means I need to be the leader."

I frown. "That doesn't sound like a good reason."

Lulu laughs through her tears. "It's not, is it?"

I stretch out my legs and flex my toes. My muscles are sore from swimming so far. "You know on land, fourteen-year-olds don't need to have life figured out."

"No?" Lulu asks.

"There's still the rest of high school and then college and then who knows what," I explain.

"You don't know what you want to do, either?" Lulu asks.

I shake my head. "Maybe be a doctor?" I say.

"That makes sense with your healing powers," Lulu says.

"I don't have the same powers on land. But I think I'd like healing people," I say.

"Yeah," Lulu says. We are silent for a few moments.

"So the mer don't have elections? For a new leader?" I ask.

"Not really. Usually a leader emerges," Lulu says. "My mom has been leading the tribe for years. At some point she might decide to do something else. Or the tribe might remove her if they don't like what she's doing."

"Is that why Storm is so worried about getting kicked out?" I interrupt. I think about the conversation I overhead between him and Ani.

"Yes. Fire Canyon works the same way. Once Storm leaves or is removed, they'll find a new leader," Lulu says.

"But why does your mom think it has to be you?" I ask.

"She thinks I don't have any direction. She's worried I'm going to waste my future." Lulu sighs.

"That's silly," I say.

"Thanks," Lulu says. "She thinks that because I don't know what I want to do, I must need help figuring it out."

"Do you have any ideas?" I ask.

"I like the stories," Lulu says.

I think about the feasts I've attended with the mer. At some point during the evening, some of the mer tell long stories about the past.

"You want to be a storyteller?" I ask.

"That's the thing. I don't really want to be one of the storytellers," Lulu says. "I trained with them for a while, learning the stories. I was so bored. I love the stories, but I don't want to tell them. I'm not sure what else to do, though."

I run through options in my mind. On land, Lulu would have lots of time to go to school. She could take a bunch of different classes and have lots of different jobs. The mer don't work this way, though.

Although honestly, the mer don't actually work. Ani and Storm run their tribes. But otherwise the mer float through life, telling stories and living in the ocean. A part of me likes it. It would be like summer vacation all of the time. But it could also get boring. The mer don't really do much.

Maybe that's okay though. I think about all the mornings I hate going to school. I wish we had more time to do our own things.

Whenever I complain my dad always says, "The world doesn't work that way." He's right. He and my mom both worked hard to get where they are. Still, I wish we had more time to simply be with each other.

"Why do you have to do anything?" I ask. "If the mer don't really do much, why do you have to pick?"

Lulu laughs at me. "We do more than you think, India Finch."

"What does that mean?" I ask.

"We don't have to worry about food or shelter or clothes. Well, not unless we're in the middle of a trip to the Bahamas," she says. "So we have more time to think."

"What do the mer think about?" I ask.

Lulu shrugs. "It's hard to explain. We dream about clean, safe waters. We live in harmony with our surroundings. We have to maintain the dome, after all. And we think about ourselves and our past. We dream about the future."

"Couldn't you do that as the leader too?" I ask.

"The leader of the mer makes sure the other mer have time to think. Ani's always paying attention to food supplies and monitoring reports. Her job is to make sure the mer are safe and protected. Then they can dream and think."

"Sounds kind of cool," I say. I pick up some rocks and move them between my fingers.

Lulu elbows me in the ribs. "Then you can be the leader," she says.

"Maybe," I say. The word slips out.

Lulu raises her eyebrows. "Really? Is that something you would want to do?"

I shrug. "The leader helps everyone else live well. There's something cool about that."

"It would mean living in the ocean for the rest of your life," Lulu says.

"Yeah," I say. "It would."

Lulu stretches her arms. "At least it would mean I wouldn't have to marry Evan."

The rocks I've been holding drop to the ground between us.

"What did you say?" I whisper.

"Oh, no," Lulu says.

"Marry Evan?" I ask.

My head turns toward her. She looks terrified. Her hands cover her mouth. "You're supposed to marry Evan?" I ask.

"It's not going to happen, India," Lulu says. "I don't like him like that."

I feel heat rising in my face. "Then why did you say it?" I say.

"It's nothing," Lulu protests.

"It must be something if you're acting like this," I say, gritting my teeth. "So tell me."

Lulu closes her eyes. "Ani and Storm have a plan," she starts. "To unite the tribes. When we're older, I'm supposed to marry Evan."

I can hardly speak. I'm so angry. "Why hasn't anyone told me?" I spit. "And why don't Ani and Storm just marry each other?"

"They say the tribes aren't ready for that," Lulu says. "They'd both get kicked out. But they hope that if they keep finding ways to bring the tribes together, Evan and I could unite them when we're older."

"By getting married!?" I cry.

"We're not going to do it," Lulu protests. "It's a stupid plan! I would never marry someone just to unite the tribes. Evan feels that way too," she adds. "It's no big deal."

"It if was no big deal," I begin, my words biting, "then why am I just hearing about it now? Why keep it a secret?"

"Because I knew you'd react like this!" Lulu shouts. I can hear Dana and Nari murmur from inside the cave. I can't tell if they're awake or not.

"You didn't trust me, is what you mean," I demand. "Otherwise why keep it a secret?"

Lulu throws up her hands. "We're back to where we started. Jeez, India, I'm sorry I ever mentioned it. Don't make it a bigger deal than it is."

"Don't turn this back on me!" I shout.

"Well, you're the one getting all upset about it," Lulu says.

"What. Exactly. Is. Happening?" Dana interrupts, rubbing her eyes. Nari hovers behind her. "Can we please get some sleep?"

"Yeah, you woke us up," Nari says. "What's going on with you two?"

"India found out about Ani and Storm's plan. The one where I'm supposed to marry Evan," Lulu says.

"Oh, that," Dana says.

"Wait, you both knew too?" I shriek. I feel like the the betrayal just tripled.

Nari lays a hand on my arm. "India, let's talk about it tomorrow. Get some sleep. You'll see it's not a big deal."

I stare at Lulu, who ignores me. I know I won't feel better in the morning. But I also know I'm too angry to keep fighting.

"Fine. Tomorrow we'll talk. If I feel like talking to you, that is," I say. I push off from the wall. Then I remember it's my shift, and I turn back.

"You all go to sleep, and leave me alone," I say.

No one objects. They swim away. I settle at the mouth of the cave, my thoughts keeping me awake all night.

CHAPTER 9

"Don't the Bahamas have sparkling blue water?" Dana asks.

"I've never been there," I say, only half listening. I'm spending my time glaring at Lulu, who ignores me. I can't believe none of them told me about how Lulu's supposed to marry Evan. Our big fight was three days ago. Since then, we've barely spoken.

"It's supposed to be sparkling water, though, right?" Dana says.

I turn to glance at her. She looks pale.

"I guess," I say. "I've seen movies, and the water is always sparkling."

"Hmm," Dana replies.

"Wait. Why are you asking?" I say. Dana's words are snapping me out of my mood, making me suspicious.

Dana swims closer to me. The two of us are behind Lulu and Nari. We munch on the strange seaweed, eating as much as we can handle. None of us likes the taste or the fact that it's slimy. I'm not sure how I'll explain to Grandpa why I lost weight on this trip.

"I don't think this is the Bahamas," Dana whispers. She glances at Lulu and Nari to make sure they don't hear.

I look around, cursing myself for not noticing sooner. The water is murky and dark. I shiver, realizing it's colder here than at Ice Canyon.

"You think we're lost?" I ask.

Dana nods. "We turned west a few days ago. I know Lulu wants us to go a little further west to avoid the Fire Canyon tribe. But what if she took us too far?" Dana asks.

Lulu and Nari are getting further away from us. I lower my voice anyway. “Do you think Lulu knows?” I ask.

“She might not. Or she does, and she's trying to cover. You know how she gets,” Dana says.

I do know how Lulu gets. She is stubborn and doesn't like to admit when she's wrong.

“We have to tell her,” I say.

“You do it,” Dana says.

“Why me?” I ask.

“She's already mad at you,” Dana says.

“Well, I'm mad at her too. I'm mad at all of you for not telling me about the Evan plan,” I say.

Dana rolls her eyes. “We didn't tell you because like Lulu said, there's nothing to tell. She's not going to marry Evan. And he doesn't want to marry her, either,” she says.

“Still would have been nice to know,” I say. My stomach grumbles loudly. I'm starving, which doesn't help my mood.

"Doesn't matter. Right now we need to tell Lulu we think we're lost," Dana says.

"Fine," I say.

Dana and I both speed up. We catch up with Lulu and Nari at the same time we see a set of caves ahead.

"Let's stop for a bit," I say. "I could use a break."

"Fine," Lulu says.

We swim over to the shallow caves. I pull a handful of the gross seaweed from my pack. The seaweed is gray and smells like dirty feet. Tastes like dirty feet too.

"Anyone want some?" I ask.

Everyone shakes their heads no. I wrinkle my nose and take the smallest bite possible. I almost spit it out.

"We have got to find something else to eat," Nari says.

"About that," I say. "Dana has something to ask." I cram a handful of seaweed into my mouth. It's gross, but at least I don't have to be the one to tell Lulu we're lost.

Dana is glaring at me. I shrug my shoulders in a small apology. Lulu watches our wordless conversation.

"What is it?" Lulu asks.

"Um, well, it's just that . . . is it possible we're lost?" Dana asks. Her voice goes all squeaky at the end.

Nari gasps. "Lost? Are we lost?"

Lulu's frown deepens. She doesn't look surprised by Dana's question. Maybe she already knew we were lost.

"We're not technically lost," Lulu says.

"Not technically lost?" Nari asks. "What does that mean?"

"Well, it means we're still in the ocean. And we're still heading south," Lulu says. Then her face falls. To everyone's surprise, she starts crying. Tears slide down her face, only to be washed away by the sea.

Nari is the first to put her arms around Lulu. Lulu turns and buries her head in Nari's shoulder.

"I'm sorry!" Lulu is sobbing now. "I thought I was taking us on a southwest path. Instead I have no idea where we are."

"Why didn't you tell us sooner?" I ask. I move closer to Lulu and put my hand on her shoulder to comfort her. Dana swims closer and takes Lulu's hand.

"I can't make sense of the stars," Lulu says. "I thought I knew which ones to follow. The angles are all wrong, though. I got confused." She sniffs and raises her head to look at us. "And I got us lost."

"We can fix it," I say.

"How are we going to fix it?" Lulu asks.

"We go to the surface and look at the sky," I say. "It's the middle of the afternoon. We just need to see where the sun is. Since it sets in the west, we'll know which way to go."

"It's cloudy today," Nari points out.

"I'm still going to look," I say. "Maybe it will be bright enough to tell where the sun is at. Stay here. I'll be right back."

"I'll go with you," Dana says.

We swim out of the caves into the cold water. I kick my legs, and Dana snaps her tail. We shoot straight up toward the surface of the water. Right below the surface, Dana takes my hand.

"I know the change can be rough for you," she says.

Dana is right. The change is always rough. We break the surface. My lungs burn as I take my first breaths of air. My eyes have a hard time adjusting to the light.

"There you go. It's okay," Dana is saying. She's still holding my hand. Her other arm is around my shoulder. "Take another breath. That's it."

"How do you stand it?" I ask. Dana often visits the shore, usually to bring me a seaweed wreath.

"You get used to it," Dana says. "How are you feeling?"

"Better," I say. "Thanks."

"No problem," Dana says.

We look overhead. All I see is a huge, empty sky. I've been to Montana on vacation. The sky is huge there too. Unlike the Montana sky, this sky feels heavy. I feel like I'm going to be crushed by it.

I look down, but all I see is water. Waves surround us. The only color I see is gray. I don't know why, but the sight makes me panic.

"I can't breathe," I gasp. Fear bubbles up inside. My face feels hot, and then ice washes over me. I start to slide beneath the surface. My arms and hands kick wildly.

Dana's hands are under my shoulders. She hauls me to the surface.

"It's going to be okay, India," she murmurs in my ear. "I've got you."

She places my hands on her shoulders and talks me through my fears.

"Focus on the horizon," Dana says. "Look at the line where the sky meets the water."

I follow her directions. At first I can't see the horizon because the water and the sky are almost the same color. Then I notice a line of brightness. As I watch, the line gets lighter. I start to feel calmer.

"That's it," Dana says. "Relax."

We float in the water for a while. The breeze touches my face. I'd almost forgotten how nice it is to feel the wind on my skin. Suddenly the horizon glows bright pink. The sun peeks through the clouds as it sets. Shades of red streak across the sky. The clouds turn rose and then purple. Eventually the light fades.

"The clouds won't let us see the stars, but at least we know which way is west," Dana says. She releases me, and I tread water next to her.

"Thanks," I say. I feel a little embarrassed that Dana saw me freaking out.

"No problem," she says. She swims closer to me. "What made you so afraid?"

I brush dripping strands of hair from my face. "Nothing," I say. "It just hit me how alone we are out here." I don't tell Dana the real reason I freaked out. The emptiness of the sky and water made me feel small. Like I didn't matter.

Dana nods but doesn't say anything. "How are you feeling now?"

"Better. I'm glad we know which way we're going now," I say.

The sky around us is getting dark.

"We should go tell Lulu and Nari we know where to go," Dana says.

"Good idea," I say.

We're about to dive beneath the water again when Dana stops me.

"I know what it's like to feel alone," she says. "It's why I go to the shore all the time."

"But there are always other mer around. You still feel alone?" I ask.

"Yeah," Dana says, blushing. "Sometimes I feel like I don't fit. But when I look at humans . . ." Her voice trails off.

"You feel like you'd fit with people?" I ask.

Dana looks embarrassed. "Don't tell Nari or Lulu, but I dream about what my life would be like if I could live on land."

My eyebrows shoot to my hairline. I spend so much time thinking about being a mermaid that it never occurred to me that one of the mermaids thinks about being human.

"What would you do if you were human?" I ask.

"I'm not sure. What I see of human life looks a lot like mer life," Dana says.

"Really?" I ask.

"People sit around and watch the water, mainly," Dana says.

I laugh. "You're only seeing humans on vacation. Believe me, it's not always like that."

We dive beneath the surface, heading back to Lulu and Nari. Along the way, I tell Dana about life on land. I've told her a lot of details already, but she always likes to hear more. On the trip back, I describe different kinds of jobs that humans have. We are almost back at the cave when she decides she might want to be a photographer.

"All we need to do is find you a waterproof camera," I say. "You'd be —"

Something moves behind Dana's shoulder, and the words die in my throat.

"What is it?" Dana asks, turning around. We are deep beneath the surface now. It's almost dark.

"Nothing," I say. "I thought I saw something move. It was probably just some fish."

"You sure?" Dana asks.

I'm about to tell her what I thought I saw, but I'm interrupted by Lulu and Nari.

"You're back!" they shout, coming to hug us.

I tell myself to relax and count my blessings. We're all safe and sound. Tomorrow we can plan a new route south. We might even find better seaweed to eat. Everything will be fine. Everyone is happy for the first time in days. I don't want to spoil it. So I don't tell them that for a moment, I thought I saw a shark over Dana's shoulder.

CHAPTER 10

Despite our new route, the three of us are still lost two days later.

"I don't understand," Dana says. "We saw the sun set. I know we're going south."

"Maybe we got turned around when we came back to the cave," I say. "It was getting dark."

"It's getting dark now," Nari says.

I can hear her teeth chattering. The water is freezing. If we had been going the right direction, we would have reached the Bahamas by now.

"We need to find a place to stop for the night," I suggest.

"We've been looking for the past hour," Dana replies. "There's nothing out here."

She's right. We are in a strange part of the ocean where there are no rock formations. No caves or places to find shelter.

"What are we going to do?" Nari asks. The rest of us tense as she asks the question no one wants to answer.

Lulu is the first one to answer. "We need to keep going," she says.

We're too tired to protest.

"And we all stick together," Lulu says.

"No one was leaving, Lu," Nari says.

Lulu looks at us. Her face softens. "I know. I didn't want anyone to get ideas about splitting up."

Nari swims over to Lulu and takes her hand. "We're safer together."

Dana takes Lulu's other hand. "Together," she says.

I take Dana's outstretched hand. "Together," I repeat. I try to ignore the dark waters closing around us. I can feel something out there, watching us. Following us.

The more I think about it, the more I'm certain I saw a shark two days ago over Dana's shoulder. Sharks hunt and eat mermaids. My friends have told me stories about sharks following mer for miles and miles, just waiting to attack. One of the reasons the mer live in tribes is for protection against sharks.

Even worse, the shark I saw looked like a great white. Great white sharks are the biggest and deadliest sharks in the ocean. They have huge teeth and can swim much faster than mermaids. If one is following us, we don't stand much of a chance against it. Our only hope is that our combined powers can prevent an attack.

We hold hands and swim into the shadowy waters. I feel eyes watching us. I can't shake the memory of the last time I felt someone watching me.

It happened the summer I was twelve. I had been at the county fair with my friend Sasha.

I walked her home and then went the last few blocks on my own. We had stayed out a little too late, and it was dark. My parents were going to be mad. To make matters worse, my phone was dead, so I couldn't call them.

I don't remember when I first noticed the car following me. The headlights were off, so maybe that's what I noticed first. The car followed me for two blocks, driving too slowly.

I turned down a random street. The car turned after me. I made another turn. So did the car. I was jogging by this point. The car sped up. It was a basic tan sedan. I didn't recognize it.

By this point I was running. I remember my legs feeling like jelly. Fear clutched my throat. I heard myself sob. Then the car sped up to match my pace.

Terrified, I tore down someone's side yard. A house loomed before me. I recognized Mrs. Olivia's big rose garden. Mrs. Olivia had been my second grade teacher. I pounded on the back door until a key turned in the lock, and I spilled into a kitchen of warmth and safety.

Mrs. Olivia called the police and then called my parents. The police scanned the roads for hours. They never found the car. I never saw it again, either.

That car is the reason I never walk home alone after dark. That car is why I check the locks on the door at night, even though I know my dad and mom have already checked. That car is also why I am convinced something is following us now.

"I don't like this," Nari whispers.

"What's to like?" Dana replies.

The water is almost dark by now. We see no sign of a cave or rocks or even a coral reef where we can rest.

"Keep going, keep going, keep going, keep going," Lulu murmurs to herself.

I feel Nari's hand tremble in mine.

"We'll be fine," I say. My words sound hollow. We all know I'm lying.

Swish!

The movement comes from behind. One moment Nari is looking at me, and the next she's gone.

I start screaming.

"What's happening?" Dana cries.

I'm no longer holding anyone's hand. The water is swirling around me, and I can't see a thing.

"Nari!" I shout.

I hear an echoing cry. Was that Nari or one of the other mermaids?

"Where is she?" Lulu shouts.

"There!" I point to a swirl of water.

"No, there!" Dana yells, pointing in the opposite direction.

The water is so dark that we can't see anything.

"We need to find her," Lulu says.

The words have just left her mouth when something swoops past us again. It's the shark. I know it. I don't see it so much as hear it. I've never been in a tornado, but everyone says they sound like trains. So do sharks.

Whoosh!

Something streaks past me. I see a glimpse of sharp white teeth and a gray fin. I shriek as it passes by me, heading for Lulu.

I lurch after it. But at the last minute its tail swings toward me and catches me in the chest.

I don't know that I've ever felt pain like this before. I double over. I can't breathe. Around me I hear my friends yelling and shouting. I can't see a thing. I don't know where anyone is. I'm terrified and in pain.

Are you a mermaid or aren't you? Grandpa's voice echoes in my head.

"Good point," I manage to squeak to no one in particular. I put my hands on my ribs and channel healing energy into my own body.

My lungs are tattered. I feel like elephants are sitting on my chest. I wonder if I've punctured a lung. I draw deep breaths of water and try to focus my mind. The pain lessens.

"Lulu! Nari! Dana!" I shout. I double over again, coughing. I can barely move. I can't see my friends at all.

I hear another whooshing sound behind me. The shark is back, and it's coming for me. I won't be able to get out of the way in time. This is the end.

Then strong hands close over my shoulders. An unfamiliar voice sounds in my ear.

"Are you okay?" the voice asks.

I nod my head, too shaken to speak.

"Stay here," the voice says.

Hands fall from my shoulder. Did I just see a tail? I squint through the dark waters. I can just make out the form of a mermaid swimming away. I follow her.

My heart stops when I see the sight in front of me. Lulu and Dana both have their hands outstretched. Currents of water swirl from Lulu's fingers. Dana is next to her, making the currents thick. Dana sets up a barrier between us and the creature that attacked us.

The shark is huge. It's larger than all of us mermaids combined. Beady eyes stare us down as it thrashes in the water. Its mouth is open. I can see rows and rows of pointed teeth waiting to taste mermaid flesh.

Dana and Lulu are holding off the shark. But even as I watch, the distance closes. My friends won't be able to hold it off for much longer.

A flicker of movement catches my eyes. Nari floats behind Lulu. My heart gives a leap when I see her.

"Nari!" I scream.

Her eyes are closed. Her body is limp. Blood pours from her shoulder, creating a cloud of red in the water.

I start to swim closer.

"Not yet," a voice says. The mermaid from before is swimming next to me. She has rosy skin and long, reddish gold hair.

"I have to help Nari," I say.

"I know," the mermaid says. "Let me help, first."

I sneak around to the other side, trying to reach Nari. From this angle, I can see that Lulu is holding onto Nari with one hand as she directs the currents toward the shark. Lulu's arms are shaking. My friends won't last much longer.

Suddenly a loud voice fills the sea.

"You have no business here, shark," the voice says. I realize it is the strange mermaid who is speaking. "You will leave," she continues.

The shark doesn't notice her. Instead it beats its tail against the current, lunging toward my friends. It's almost within arm's length.

The mermaid swims closer. She raises her hands high above her head. Then she pulls her arms down through the water, bringing her hands together.

BOOM!

Everything goes white, then gray, and then black. All sound is gone. I tumble through the water, blind and confused. I reach out for something, anything. Hands grab me again.

"Sorry about that," a voice says in my ear. "The shark is gone."

I look into the face of the mermaid who saved us.

"Nari?" I whisper.

The mermaid nods her head. "The one with the long black hair? She's badly hurt. We'll get her to my cave and see what we can do."

"Who are you?" I ask.

"My name is Alix," she says.

Lulu edges closer. "Did you say Alix?" she asks.

"I did," the mermaid said. "Why?"

"We're from Ice Canyon," Lulu says.

Alix peers closer at us. "Ice Canyon? You must know Ani."

"She's my mom," Lulu says. "I think I've heard her talk about you before."

Alix nods. "I'm a friend of hers. You're safe here."

The edges of my vision blur. I regain focus when I see Lulu and Dana hovering over Alix's shoulder. They look scared.

"Stay with me," Alix says. "We need to help your friend."

"Okay," I say, even though I am dazed.

Then I see that Lulu and Dana are carrying Nari between them. Nari's face looks gray. Bite marks dot her arm. Blood is pumping from her wounds. The sight brings me back to myself.

I hold out my hands and start channeling healing energy into Nari's injuries.

"Let's go," I say.

CHAPTER 11

I don't remember the trip to Alix's cave. My attention is on Nari. At one point Lulu puts her arm around my waist so I won't have to swim. I'm able to focus all of my energy on Nari.

The trip takes forever, but suddenly we are there. We lay Nari on a stone bench. I do not take my hands from her shoulder. Her blood pulses between my fingers.

"How is she?" Lulu asks.

I shake my head. "I can't get the bleeding to stop," I say.

Nari's pulse flutters beneath my fingers. She is starting to slip away.

I swallow a lump in my throat. "We're losing her," I say.

No one speaks. Lulu and Dana are holding onto each other for dear life. Alix swims behind us, rummaging in a shallow indentation in the cave wall.

"Here," she says, swimming back to me. She presses something into my hand.

"What is it?" I ask.

"It's a mixture of kelp and a few other ingredients. It will help stop the bleeding," Alix explains.

I don't know if I should trust her or not, but Nari's wounds aren't healing. I take Alix's bundle of seaweed.

"What do I do with it?" I ask.

"Press it into her wounds," Alix says.

"Is it safe?" Lulu asks.

"It's our only chance to slow the bleeding enough so your friend can finish healing her," Alix says.

"My name is India," I say, glancing at Alix.

Alix nods. "Nice to meet you, India. I wish it was under different circumstances."

I press the seaweed into Nari's skin.

"Press hard," Alix says.

"I know," I say. "I took first aid last semester. Always apply pressure to a wound."

Alix probably has no idea what I'm talking about. Mermaids don't have first aid classes or semesters. If Alix is confused by my words, though, she doesn't say anything. She is remarkably calm, considering a group of ragged mermaids — plus one humanish mermaid — just landed on her doorstep.

"Is it working?" Dana asks. Her voice is rusty.

I lessen the pressure for a moment. The bleeding is slowing. "I think so," I say.

"Keep applying pressure," Alix says.

We stay like this for a long time. I'm holding the seaweed to Nari's skin while also channeling healing energy. Lulu and Dana hold each other. Alix watches all of us.

"It's working," I finally whisper.

I remove my hands slowly. The bleeding has stopped. Nari's pulse is weak but steady. A little color has returned to her face.

Alix bends over Nari. "She's looking better," she says. "Now she'll need to rest. So will you," she says to me.

I let my hands fall from Nari. She doesn't wake up.

"There's nothing more we can do for her now," Alix says, herding us into another room. "We should talk."

Dana refuses to go. "I'm staying with Nari," she says, her voice fierce.

"Okay," Lulu says. We can tell Dana will not be moved.

Lulu and I follow Alix to the next room. We float near the doorway so we can keep an eye on Nari and Dana.

Alix's eyes soften when she sees us. She looks like she would cup Lulu's cheek if she were close enough. "My dear, you're the spitting image of Ani," she says. "Tell me, how is Ice Canyon these days?"

"How do you know Ani exactly?" Lulu asks.

"I knew her when we were young, before the mer moved to the canyons. We lived near Florida," Alix says. Her eyes get a faraway look. "Those were wonderful days."

"What happened?" Lulu asks.

"Florida was too dangerous. We lived too close to the coast. Well, the humans were getting too close to us," Alix corrects. She looks at me. "No offense."

"None taken," I say.

"There were two or three times when a mermaid was almost photographed," Alix continues. "After that, most of the mer moved to the canyons."

"Why didn't you?" Lulu asks.

"I was happiest by myself," Alix says. "Some of us are like that. I moved here. I keep in touch with the Ice Canyon mer, though."

"How?" I ask. The mer don't have a postal system, and they certainly don't have email.

"There are others like me," Alix says. "Other mer who live by themselves. We keep an eye out for each other. News from the canyons filters down here from time to time."

"Um," I clear my throat. "Can you tell us where 'here' is, exactly?"

Alix looks surprised. "Are you lost?"

"Well, kind of," I say. I glance at Lulu, who is pressing her lips together. She's still upset about getting us lost.

"But aren't you here for the trident?" Alix asks.

If I were sitting in a chair, I would have fallen out of it. We gape at Alix. Even Dana peeks her head around the corner.

"How did you know about the trident?" Lulu asks.

"I'd heard rumors that the trident was near Rose Island. I figured it would only be a few months before someone came looking for it," Alix says.

"So we're close?" I ask.

"Yes," Alix says. "You're a half day's swim from Rose Island, at most."

I turn to Lulu. "We made it," I say.

Lulu has a few tears in her eyes. I realize how hard the journey has been on her. She took responsibility for getting us to Rose Island, which wasn't easy.

"We made it," she repeats.

"We made it," Dana says, sliding into the room. The three of us start hugging each other. We are laughing and crying at the same time.

"Can you take us there?" Lulu asks Alix once we calm down.

"I will, if you wish," she says. "I have to say, however, that I'm surprised Ani sent you by yourselves. It's a dangerous trip."

We all look anywhere except at Alix.

"I see," Alix says, reading the guilt in our faces. "This is an unapproved trip, is it?"

"Yeah," I say. "But please, can you take us?"

"If we don't get it, the Fire Canyon mer will get it," Lulu says. "They'll use it to cause major damage to the coasts."

"Storm wants to create tidal waves, does he?" Alix says.

"You know Storm?" I ask.

"Well enough," Alix says. She bites the inside of her cheek. "I suppose this changes things."

"So you'll take us?" Dana asks.

"I suppose that depends on what you'll do with the trident once you get it," Alix says.

"We're going to take it home to my mother," Lulu says.

Alix frowns. "How did you know about the trident and Rose Island in the first place?" she asks.

I squirm. "That was me," I confess. "I overheard Storm telling Ani about the trident. He talked about how his tribe wants to use it to create tidal waves and hurricanes."

"He told Ani about his plans?" Alix asks.

"I'm not sure Storm wants to use the trident," I say.

"I see," Alix says, looking thoughtful.

"We think he was telling my mom so she could send a group to get the trident too," Lulu says.

"And did she?" Alix asks.

"Um, she was thinking about it," Lulu says.

"But you decided to take matters into your own hands," Alix says.

"Yes," Lulu says.

"And look where it got you," Alix says, gesturing to where Nari is lying on the table. Her eyes are still closed.

"That's not fair," Lulu says. "We didn't want Nari to get hurt."

"No one ever wants to get hurt," Alix says. "But you didn't understand how dangerous the journey would be."

"I guess not," Dana says, hanging her head. Curtains of red hair fall around her face.

Alix sighs. "Here's what we're going to do. I will take you to Rose Island tomorrow to see the trident. We will let your friend rest. Once she's well enough to travel, I will take you all home."

"But —" Lulu says.

"No buts," Alix interrupts her. "This is my best offer. Now do you agree?"

We have no choice. We all nod.

"Good. Now let's get you some food and tuck you into bed."

CHAPTER 12

The next morning, Nari wakes up. She eats a little bit of seaweed and then falls asleep again. The seaweed is sweeter here, so we all felt better after we ate.

Now that we know Nari will be okay, Alix takes Lulu and me to Rose Island. Dana volunteers to stay with Nari while the rest of us get the trident.

The waters near Rose Island are lovely and blue. We swim past coral reefs of dazzling color. Tiny fish dart in and out. If it were a different day, I would chase them.

"I'm glad your friend is better," Alix says as we float through warm waters.

"So are we," I say.

"You are a very talented healer," Alix tells me.

"Thanks," I say. I'm suddenly very aware of my legs. "Um, were you surprised to see someone like me?"

"You mean part-mer and part-human?" Alix asks.

I nod.

"There have always been ones like you," she says.

"Do you know others like me?" I ask.

Alix shakes her head. "There aren't many like you. Mer and humans don't always mix well. And most of you stay on land."

"Why?" I ask.

Alix shrugs. "I suspect it is easier to blend in with humans than with the mer."

"Oh," I say. I feel oddly disappointed.

"How did you get rid of the shark yesterday?" Lulu asks, interrupting my thoughts.

"That's my gift," Alix says. "I can create sonic booms. I don't do it often," she adds. "But it was fun to do."

"I can imagine," Lulu says.

"We're almost at Rose Island," Alix says. She gestures to a spot in front of us. I realize that the earth is sloping up to us. I can see the sandy bottom emerge through the depths.

"Why is the trident here?" I ask.

"Pirates," Alix says.

I start to laugh but stop when I realize she isn't joking. "Seriously?" I ask.

"Legend says the trident was captured by pirates centuries ago. They buried their treasures off the coast of Rose Island, but they didn't bury it deep enough. The water finally washed away the sand."

We are surrounded by sea turtles and schools of electric blue fish. A pod of dolphins swims past. One nudges Alix, and she scratches its head before it swims away.

For a second I let myself enjoy where I am. "This is beautiful," I say.

Lulu's arm shoots across my chest, bringing me up short.

"Not so beautiful now, is it?" she says.

I look where she's pointing.

There, at the point where the bottom of the ocean slopes up to meet the island, lies a treasure chest. The chest is open. Gold coins and twinkling rubies spill from the chest.

Surrounding the chest are two groups of mer.

I recognize one group. Five mer from Ice Canyon. I can't see their faces well, but these must be the mer Ani sent. Six other mer face them across the treasure chest. They are from Fire Canyon. I recognize Storm's shaggy head and wide shoulders among the group.

My heart is in my throat. I look around for Evan. My breath catches when I see him. He's with the Fire Canyon mer, near the back of the group.

Evan is the first one to notice us. His head lifts as if he could sense me looking at him. I'm surprised by what I see flashing across his face. His eyes widen when he sees me. He looks angry and then scared. For a second I think I see something like hope in his face and then maybe sorrow.

"They already have it," Lulu whispers. I look back at the treasure chest.

Even from here I can see the trident. One of the Fire Canyon mer is holding it. I'm not sure what all the fuss is about. The trident is about five feet long. Three pointy spikes stick up from one end. The trident isn't even pretty. The color is dull silver. I don't know why I expect it to be solid gold and covered in diamonds.

"What are we doing to do?" Lulu asks me.

I turn to Alix. "Can't you use your sonic boom to stun them?"

Alix shakes her head. "I only use those powers if there are no other options. Let's go talk to them first."

We can hear the argument as we approach.

"The trident is ours!" the mermaid holding the trident shouts.

The Ice Canyon mer are shaking their heads. "You will not use it properly," a voice is saying.

I recognize that voice. So does Lulu.

"Mom?" Lulu asks, swimming forward.

All of the mer notice us. Ani gives a soft shriek and flies to Lulu.

"There you are, my foolish girl," she says, folding Lulu into a huge hug. She pulls me into the embrace with one arm. "And India Finch. What will your grandfather say once he finds out where you've been?"

"Um, I was thinking that maybe I wouldn't tell him?" I say.

Ani shakes her head. "What were you girls thinking?" she asks. "You could have been hurt. Killed." Her voice breaks as she hugs Lulu again.

"Mom," Lulu protests, but she doesn't pull away from Ani's hug.

"Where are Nari and Dana?" Ani asks. Her face goes pale.

"They're okay," I say. "Nari got hurt, but she'll be fine. Dana's staying with her."

From the look on her face, Ani has a thousand questions.

"They've had quite the time of it," Alix says.

Ani notices the mermaid. A smile of disbelief spreads across her face. "Alix? I wondered if I'd see you here. It's been too long."

"It has," Alix says. She and Ani grip hands. It is clear they are friends.

"This is all very touching, but we have to figure out what to do with the trident," Storm says. His voice sounds like thunder on the waves.

"Storm. You haven't changed a bit," Alix comments.

Storm nods at the mermaid, but he won't be distracted. "There will be time to catch up later," he mutters.

"There's not time now," I interrupt. "Look."

The mermaid with the trident has been edging away from the group. When everyone turns to look, she stops, clutching the trident to her chest. Her orange tail flicks back and forth.

"This belongs to us," she says.

"You have no claim to it, Ellie," Ani says. "Not any more than the rest of us."

"We cannot give it to you," Ellie says. "You will only hide it away. What we need is to create storms. The mer will only be safe when humans are no more."

"There are too many of us," I say. Everyone's heads turn to me. "A tidal wave, no matter how big, won't get rid of seven billion humans."

"It will be a start," Ellie says. "Tell her, Storm."

Storm stares at the trident in Ellie's hands. Then he sighs. "She's right," he says.

"Who's right?" I ask. "Me or her?"

Storm doesn't answer right away. I'm watching him so I don't notice the moment when Evan swims over to me. Suddenly his hand is surrounding mine. Our fingers are interlaced, and he's squeezing my palm. I feel as if light is shining out of the top of my head.

"Yeah, Dad," Evan asks. "Who's right? Are we going to harm humans, or are we going to find a way to live in peace?"

Storm watches his son for a long moment. His lips soften. I remember his words to Ani in her cave. Storm himself wasn't sure if they should use the trident or not.

For a second I think he's going to agree with me. Then he shakes his head. "We cannot live in peace with humans." His eyes bore into mine. "Ever."

At his words, all of the mer spring into action. Ellie starts swimming away with the trident. The other Fire Canyon mer set up a shield between us and her. Powers start flying everywhere as the mermaids unleash their gifts. Soon the water is a churning mess.

Ellie is at the center of the battle, holding the trident with one hand as she turns the water black around her, creating confusion. Sparks of power are shooting from the tips of the trident, like bits of electricity.

I can feel the water starting to pulse and stir in response. If we aren't careful, the trident will cause a tidal wave while we're fighting over it.

Fins and arms are flying everywhere. Some of the mermaids are thickening the water while others are drawing sand from the bottom of the ocean to send at each other in thick curtains. The water is boiling hot and then freezing cold.

I'm bumped from behind. Evan's arm slides around my waist. "Are you okay?" he shouts in my ear.